A NOTE TO PARENTS

When your children are ready to "step into reading," giving them the right books is as crucial as giving them the right food to eat. **Step into Reading Books** present exciting stories and information reinforced with lively, colorful illustrations that make learning to read fun, satisfying, and worthwhile. They are priced so that acquiring an entire library of them is affordable. And they are beginning readers with a difference—they're written on five levels.

Early Step into Reading Books are designed for brand-new readers, with large type and only one or two lines of very simple text per page. **Step 1 Books** feature the same easy-to-read type as the Early Step into Reading Books, but with more words per page. **Step 2 Books** are both longer and slightly more difficult, while **Step 3 Books** introduce readers to paragraphs and fully developed plot lines. **Step 4 Books** offer exciting nonfiction for the increasingly independent reader.

The grade levels assigned to the five steps—preschool through kindergarten for the Early Books, preschool through grade 1 for Step 1, grades 1 through 3 for Step 2, grades 2 through 3 for Step 3, and grades 2 through 4 for Step 4—are intended only as guides. Some children move through all five steps very rapidly; others climb the steps over a period of several years. Either way, these books will help your child "step into reading" in style!

To Eric Siegel

Text copyright © 1996 by
Lucille Recht Penner.
Illustrations copyright © 1996
by Kazushige Nitta. All rights
reserved under International and
Pan-American Copyright
Conventions. Published in the
United States by Random House,
Inc., New York, and simultaneously
in Canada by Random House of Canada
Limited, Toronto.

http://www.randomhouse.com/

*Library of Congress Cataloging-in-Publication
Data*
Penner, Lucille Recht. Twisters! / by Lucille Recht
Penner ; illustrated by Kazushige Nitta.
p. cm. — (Step into reading. Step 2 book)
Summary: Describes how tornadoes and hurricanes
form and the damage they do.
ISBN 0-679-88271-5 (trade) — ISBN 0-679-98271-X
(lib. bdg.) 1. Tornadoes—Juvenile literature. [1. Tornadoes.
2. Hurricanes.] I. Nitta, Kazushige, ill. II. Title. III. Series.
QC955.2.P46 1996 551.5'53—dc20 96-19352
Printed in the United States of America

10 9 8 7 6 5 4 3 2 1

STEP INTO READING is a trademark of Random House, Inc.

Step into Reading™

TWISTERS!

by Lucille Recht Penner
illustrated by Kazushige Nitta

A Step 2 Book

Random House 🏠 New York

On a summer afternoon,
a train chugged through fields
of golden wheat.
Suddenly, thunder crashed.
A whirling black cloud
swooped down toward the tracks.

The engineer
looked out his window.
That whirling cloud
was a twister,
and he was heading
right into it!
It was too late
to stop!

The twister ripped off
the cab's steel roof.
Wind clawed at the man.
He grabbed his chair,
closed his eyes,
and held on.

Suddenly, the wind stopped.

The engineer opened his eyes.

The sky was clear.

The train had passed

right through the twister!

That twister was a tornado.

A tornado is one of the strongest forces
on Earth.

It can pick up
a car or a house.

Tornadoes can even rip
somebody's clothes off.

The United States
has more tornadoes
than anywhere else.
Most of them
hit the Midwest
in an area called Tornado Alley.
This is a place where cold air
coming down from Canada
collides with warm air
coming up from
the Gulf
of Mexico.

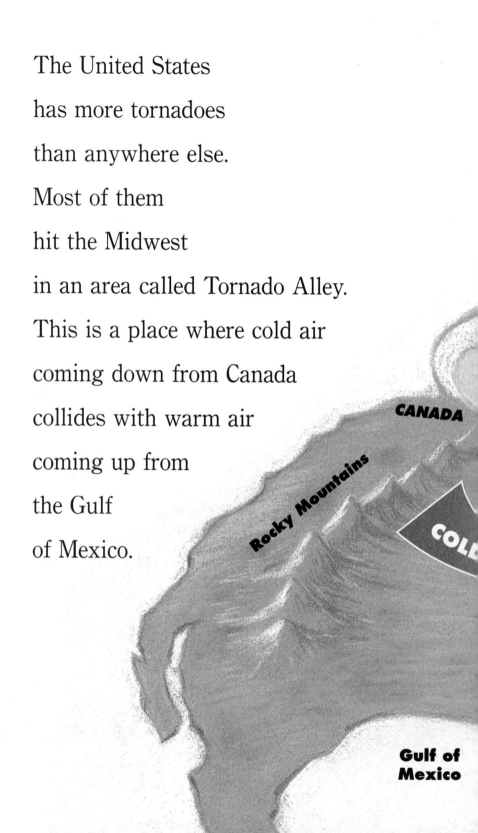

CANADA

Rocky Mountains

COLD

Gulf of
Mexico

As the warm air rises,
it punches a hole
in the cold air.
Up the warm air swirls
in a long column.

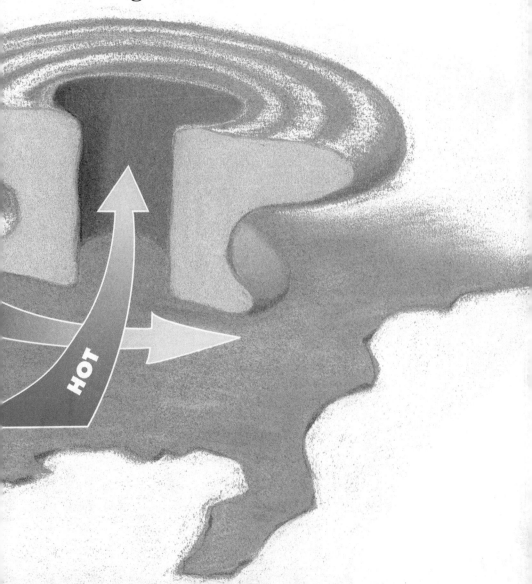

The column of swirling air
begins to look
like a funnel
hanging from the sky.

If the funnel
touches the ground,
it's a tornado.

Tornadoes seem crazy.
Sometimes they smash
whatever they touch.
But once a tornado
lifted a crate of eggs
and carried it
half a mile.
It put the crate
down gently.
Not a single egg
was broken!

Another tornado
lifted the roof
off a schoolhouse.
Children were blown
out of their chairs.
They landed hundreds
of feet away.
Luckily, no one
was badly hurt.

Most tornadoes are
over in minutes.
But one tornado
lasted four hours.
It tore up towns
along its path
through Missouri, Illinois,
and Indiana.

A farmer in Illinois
saw green paper
fall out of the sky.
It was money!
The tornado had
carried it from a town
a hundred miles away.

Most tornadoes strike
in the afternoon or early evening
in spring and summer.
The National Weather Service
issues a "tornado watch"
if there's a chance that
a tornado is likely to form.

A "tornado warning"
is more serious.
It means a tornado
has *already* formed.
The warning goes out
over radio and television.
Sirens blow and wail.
Take cover!

The safest place
to take cover
is a storm cellar.
It's a special
underground room.

If you don't
have a storm cellar,
you should go down
into your basement.
If you don't have
a basement either,
hide in a closet
with no outside walls.

One family hid in a closet

as a tornado

roared overhead.

When the wind died down,

they opened the closet door.

The rest of their house was gone!

Tornadoes can make

a loud, scary noise

like a million buzzing bees.

Most tornadoes form over land.
Twisters that form over water
are called "waterspouts."
Waterspouts can suck
all the water
out of a pond.
They can suck up
frogs, tadpoles, and fish.

A waterspout once
dropped hundreds of fish
on a town in Louisiana.
Everyone ran outside.
The streets were covered
with fresh fish.
Some were still alive
and flopping around.

Another kind of twister
sometimes forms in the desert.
It's called a "dust devil."
Hot air rises, whipping up
a spiral of sand and dust.
It looks like someone
doing a wild dance.
Some dust devils
are little.
Some are a thousand
feet high!

In Tucson, Arizona,
a dust devil pulled
the roof off a house.
It came down
across the street.

Tornadoes, waterspouts,

and dust devils

are never more than a mile wide.

Hurricanes are much bigger.

Hurricane winds blow in circles

that can be hundreds

of miles across.

At the center

is an area

called the hurricane's "eye."

In the eye,

the air is calm.

The sun may shine.

But around it,

the wind blows

faster and faster.

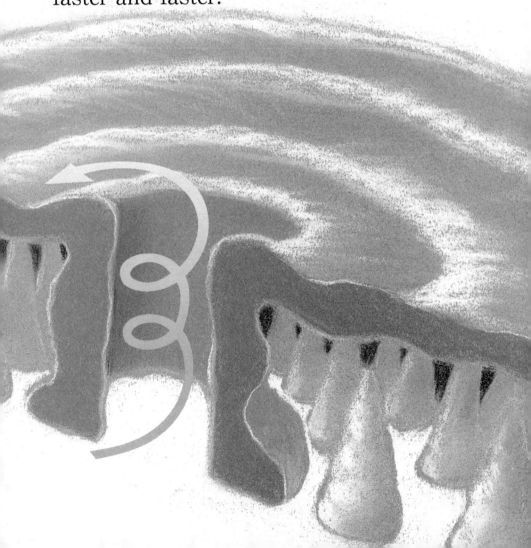

The first hurricane each year
is given a name starting
with the letter A.
The second hurricane
gets a B name.
Boys' and girls' names
take turns.
Agnes, Bob, and Carol
were all famous hurricanes.

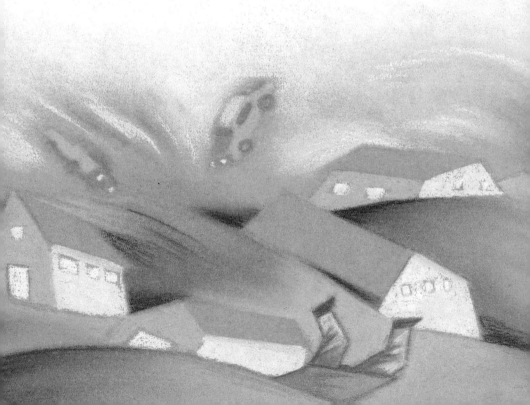

Hurricanes form over oceans.

Their powerful winds

push the sea into waves.

The water swells up in a huge bump

called a storm surge.

When a hurricane comes ashore,

the storm surge can

wash away beaches.

It can even

cut islands in half!

In 1900, a great storm
struck Galveston, Texas.
The wind rose suddenly.
People stood on the beach,
amazed at the sight
of the huge waves.

Isaac Cline,
the chief weather forecaster,
raced up and down
with a horse and buggy.

"Get back," he shouted.

"It's a hurricane!"

Suddenly, the storm surge
swept over the beach
and poured into the city.
More than 6,000 people
died in the storm.

The dead bodies of people and animals
floated through the streets.

Isaac Cline's warning
had come too late.

Now the National Weather Service
tracks hurricanes
with weather satellites.

It warns people

to leave the coast

if a hurricane is coming.

Shelters are set up

in buildings inland.

People can stay there

until the storm passes.

In 1969, the Weather Service

issued a warning.

Hurricane Camille was coming!

Thousands of people fled inland.

The early warning saved their lives.

But people in one apartment house

decided to stay

and watch the storm.

They were going to have

a hurricane party.

In the middle of the party,

Camille's winds smashed into land

at 170 miles per hour!

Its storm surge

destroyed the building.

There was only

one survivor.

In 1992, part of Florida
was changed forever.
Hurricane Andrew
washed away beaches,
knocked down bridges,
and wiped out whole towns.

But almost everyone escaped.
Again, the warning
had come in time.
Although Andrew destroyed
thousands of homes,
only 39 people were killed.

Twisters are scary.
Most people run away
from them.
But "storm chasers"
want to see
storms close-up
and photograph them.
Storm chasers drive vans
with video cameras
on the roof.

If a tornado
gets too close,
the vans can go
very fast.

It's dangerous work!
Only an expert
should chase a tornado.

Air force pilots
fly right into hurricanes
to measure their
size, speed, and direction.
They fly special planes
called "hurricane hunters."

It's strange inside
a hurricane.
Sometimes the pilot
doesn't even know
if he's right side up
or upside down.
He can only tell
from his instruments.

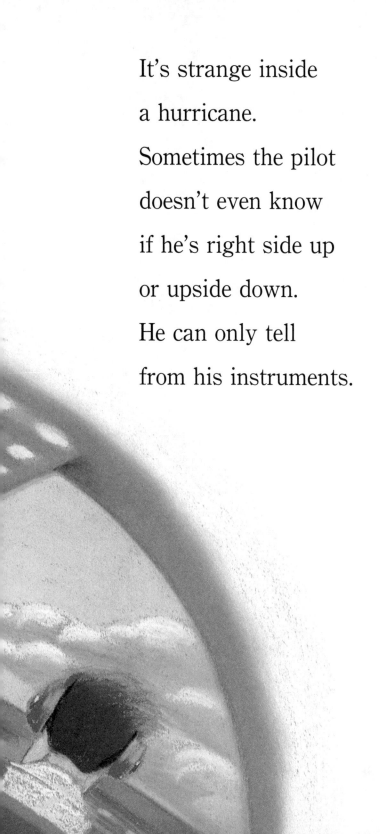

A tornado can
knock down buildings
faster than a
wrecker's ball.

A great hurricane
has the power
of a hydrogen bomb.

Scientists,
hurricane hunters,
and storm chasers
are learning the secrets
of twisters and hurricanes.
And the more we know,
the safer we will be.